KT-416-406

The
CHOCOLATE
Dog

WITHDRAWN

KT 2110877 3

Look out for more books by Holly Webb

A Cat Called Penguin

For younger readers:

Magic Molly
1. The Witch's Kitten
2. The Wish Puppy
3. The Invisible Bunny
4. The Secret Pony
5. The Shy Piglet
6. The Good Luck Duck

For slightly older readers:

The Animal Magic stories
1. Catmagic
2. Dogmagic
3. Hamstermagic
4. Rabbitmagic
5. Birdmagic
6. Ponymagic
7. Mousemagic

www.holly-webb.com

The CHOCOLATE Dog

HOLLY WEBB

Illustrated by Sharon Rentta

SCHOLASTIC

First published in the UK in 2012 by Scholastic Children's Books
An imprint of Scholastic Ltd
Euston House, 24 Eversholt Street
London, NW1 1DB, UK
Registered office: Westfield Road, Southam, Warwickshire, CV47 0RA
SCHOLASTIC and associated logos are trademarks and/
or registered trademarks of Scholastic Inc.

Text copyright © Holly Webb, 2012
Illustration copyright © Sharon Rentta, 2012

The rights of Holly Webb and Sharon Rentta to be identified as the author
and illustrator of this work have been asserted by them.

Cover illustration © Sharon Rentta, 2012

ISBN 978 1 407 13177 1

A CIP catalogue record for this book is
available from the British Library.
All rights reserved.
This book is sold subject to the condition that it shall not, by way
of trade or otherwise, be lent, hired out or otherwise circulated in any form
of binding or cover other than that in which it is published. No part of this
publication may be reproduced, stored in a retrieval system, or transmitted
in any form or by any means (electronic, mechanical, photocopying,
recording or otherwise) without the prior written
permission of Scholastic Limited.

Printed and bound by CPI Group (UK) Ltd, Croydon, CR0 4YY
Papers used by Scholastic Children's Books are made
from wood grown in sustainable forests.

1 3 5 7 9 10 8 6 4 2

Thi[s is a work of fiction...]
di[...]

Kingston upon Thames Libraries	
KT 2110877 3	
Askews & Holts	31-Aug-2012
JF	£4.99
∿M	30016775

For Jade, Amy and Rachel, and
Jasmine, Maddy and Faith
– two families of amazing sisters

Amy wriggled. Choc had his nose in her ear again. "Ow, Choccie, don't." She leaned away from him, giggling. "It's cold." They'd been in the car for ages, four hours at least, and the heat was making Choc's chilly nose feel icy. He'd been licking the bare part of her shoulder or sticking his nose in her ear every few minutes since they'd left the house.

Choc hated being stuck in his dog crate in the boot of the car. He saw no reason why he couldn't sit next to Amy and Lara in the back seat. He knew that was where he was meant to be – right in the middle of the two girls, so they could both make a big fuss of him. He stared through the wire of the crate with mournful chocolate-brown eyes, and slobbered down the back of Amy's vest top.

"Uurgh, Choc. . ." Amy squashed sideways so he couldn't dribble on her neck any more, and peered through the wire at him. "I know you're bored, but *please* stop licking me. . ."

Choc's eyes were round and soulful like Maltesers now, and Amy smiled. She could never resist that look. She pushed two fingers through the wire of the crate and scratched him behind the ears. He sighed with delight, leaning his head up against the side, eyes closed, shivering happily. Behind the ears was the best place. A really good behind-the-ears scratch could have him on the floor with all four paws in the air. He slumped gradually down to the floor with a long sigh.

Amy eased her hand back from the crate. Choc had fallen asleep, she thought, blinking as the air in the car slanted suddenly green. The trees were arching over the road, pushing against each other so close that the car was driving through a green tunnel, a tunnel with strange dappled patterns of sunlight here and there. Amy wondered if anyone else had noticed. Dad was only looking straight ahead. That was probably a good thing, if you were driving, Amy thought sleepily. It was the middle of the afternoon, and it felt like they'd been driving all day. Her little sister, Lara, looked like she was about to melt into her pink car seat, and their mum was fanning herself with a paper fan Amy had made her at school.

Amy leaned her head against the car window

and sighed. She was hot, and half-asleep like Choc, and the car seat was sticking to her legs. She took a breath, about to ask Mum if they were nearly there, and then caught Dad's eye in the mirror, and didn't. Everyone was grumpy, and Mum had been grumpy all week. The baby wasn't due for another month, but Amy was already feeling fed up with it, and the way it was making Mum so tired and cross.

Lara did it instead. "Mum, are we there yet?"

"No." Mum's voice was tight and tired. She shifted uncomfortably in her seat, as though she was just as sticky as Amy. And about four times the size. She was enormous.

"If we were there we'd be able to see the sea, Lara, wouldn't we?" Mum sighed.

"Not if there was something in the way,"

Lara muttered. "Like a wall. Or trees. Houses."

"Lara, don't," Dad said firmly. "Ten more minutes."

"That's what you said last time," Amy couldn't help putting in. Dad seemed to think they wouldn't notice. He'd been saying ten more minutes for ages. "Oh! Did you see? That was a sign for Sandmouth! Five, it said, five miles."

"There you are, then. Ten minutes," Dad agreed smugly. "Like I said."

"It's pink!" Amy stared at the cottage as they pulled up outside.

Her mother nodded, a little doubtfully. "When they said it was called Shrimp Cottage, I didn't realize it would be painted shrimp pink. It's a bit bright. . ."

Amy smiled. "I like it." The cottage was the same colour as pink candy shrimps, the ones on the penny sweets shelf at the sweetshop they went to after school sometimes. She loved those. She always had to save one for Choc, though, otherwise he knew she'd had them – he had a nose like a sniffer dog. If she didn't give him a shrimp, he'd sit there and howl at her until she said she was sorry.

Amy had to be very careful what she fed him. Choc didn't only have eyes like Maltesers, he'd happily wolf down half a packet of them too, and dogs weren't supposed to have chocolate; it was really bad for their insides. Choc just didn't seem to think so. Amy could understand why – after all, they *had* named him Chocolate, so why couldn't he eat it?

Mum and Amy and Lara had made an emergency appointment at the vet's last Christmas, after they'd come down in the morning and found that Choc had eaten all the chocolate Christmas decorations. And the foil, unless he'd carefully taken it off and binned it. He must have climbed on the arm of the sofa to reach the top ones, Amy reckoned.

The vet had said he thought Choc would be fine, he'd probably just be really sick, because milk chocolate wasn't as bad as the dark kind. But Choc hadn't even burped. He came home from the vet's sulking like he always did (he would duck right down in the car and try to dig his claws into the floor of his car crate if they even drove past). Then when they got in the house, he whisked past Mum, who was trying to head him off into the kitchen – she would rather he was sick on a tiled floor – and back into the living room to see if the tree had grown any more chocolate. It hadn't, so he had a peppermint candy cane instead.

Choc was whining in his car crate now. He knew they'd stopped, and he couldn't stand being shut up in the boot for much longer.

"We'd better get him out." Dad took his seat belt off and stretched wearily. "Poor dog sounds as though he's got his legs crossed. Why don't you girls take him for a quick run round that patch of grass over there? He can have a proper walk later, once we've unpacked. I need to go and pick up the keys from the cottage next door."

"Can't we go to the beach?" Amy asked hopefully, but Dad was already making for the next-door cottage.

The beach was so close – just down a long flight of stone steps on the other side of the road. Amy could hear the sea, and see it. It was almost blue. Not blue like on a postcard, where the sea was a shiny jewel colour. More of a greenish, brownish, blueish thing, heaving up and down like a blanket someone was shaking. She wanted to go and stand at the edge of it. Dip her toes in it. And she could tell Choc wanted to do the same. His ears were blowing in the sea-smelling breeze, and he kept looking up at her hopefully. Every time they went to the park, he tried to jump in the duck pond, and this was the biggest duck pond he'd ever seen. Amy crouched down next to him. "It doesn't have enormous ducks to match," she murmured, running her fingers down the curls of his ears. "But there might be fish, I suppose," she

9

added doubtfully. "Oh, and seagulls. But they look mean. I'd leave them alone."

Choc quivered with excitement. He was quite well trained – Dad had taken him to classes – so he stayed sitting, but he was sitting and leaning forward about as much as he possibly could without falling over. His nose was stretched out towards those steps. It didn't help that Lara was dancing up and down on the edge of the pavement, trying to get a better view of the sea. Her little sister wasn't as well trained as Choc, Amy thought, grinning to herself. She needed a lead more than he did.

Dad was coming back now, clutching a set of keys and a folder. Mum had been leaning against the front of the car, having a drink of water, but now she turned to look out at the sea. "Isn't it lovely?" she murmured. "We'll go down for a walk later, you two. Let's just get settled in first."

As Dad unlocked the door, the two girls raced in. There was something fascinating about the cottage – just because it was so different to home. Their house was like all the others in the street, a semi, painted white, with a square of garden at the front and a long thin strip at the back. Over the fence at the end of their back garden was another garden, and a whole street that mirrored theirs. If Amy went to tea with a friend who lived anywhere near, she pretty much knew where all the rooms were without asking. Although sometimes the stairs were on the wrong side of the hallway, which just looked weird.

Here, it was different. Shrimp Cottage was squashed up between two other houses, and neither of them matched. Inside, it opened up a little, somehow getting wider at the back, like a little burrow. Tunnels opened out here and there. The girls ran into a living room with fat, sagging sofas and a small stove in the fireplace, then a kitchen with a long wooden table, and last, a little glass sunroom full of wicker chairs, and one huge spider plant that seemed to be trying to take over the world.

A twisting wooden staircase led up to the bedrooms. A huge one for their parents, with a great big bed – Mum would be pleased. She said she needed a bed and a half now. Then there was a pretty blue-and-white room with striped wallpaper and fussy patchwork bedcovers.

"You can have this one," Amy said quickly to Lara, even though there was a view of the sea. It looked wonderful from the high window, much bluer somehow, with late afternoon sun streaming golden across it. She loved the wide window sill too. But perhaps the other room would have an even better view, and this one was just too frilly.

Mum had struggled up the stairs behind them with an armful of Lara's soft toys. "There's only one room, girls. We did say, don't you remember? We booked late; with the baby, everything was a bit disorganized. I wasn't sure I was up to going away, and then there weren't many places that would take Choc as well. The cottage *is* a bit small, but we'll manage."

Amy gaped at her. "One room? You mean I have to share with Lara?"

"I'm having this bed!" Lara bounced on to the bed by the window, seizing her mermaid doll from Mum. She sat cross-legged on the bed, clutching the doll and smirking at Amy.

"But Mum. . ." Amy gulped. She remembered now, but it hadn't seemed to matter that much a few weeks before. She'd been so excited about going on holiday that she'd forgotten it meant a whole week in the same bedroom as Lara. "She talks in her sleep!"

Her mum sighed and eased herself down on to the other bed. Amy's bed. "I know. But not very often."

"And she sleepwalks." Amy slumped down next to Mum on the bed. Her bed now. "I'll wake up and she'll be standing next to me looking all spooky. It makes me go shivery when she does that!"

Lara sniggered and made a ghostly, toothy

face at Amy.

Amy lay backwards, gazing up at the ceiling. She could hear paws scrabbling on the wooden stairs – Choc was coming to see where they'd got to.

Choc peered whiskerily round the bedroom door and flapped his ears happily at Amy and Lara.

Amy laughed. He had his red fleece blanket in his teeth, the one that usually lined his basket at home. It had been in the dog crate with him, to make him feel better about the journey. Now he gazed lovingly at Amy's mum, doing his best big-eyed look. The one that said *You know I am clean, loving and perfectly house-trained. . .*

"Where's Choc sleeping?" Amy asked thoughtfully.

15

"In the kitchen, like he does at home." Her mum sounded surprised.

"Couldn't he sleep up here with us? As a holiday treat?" She turned over, squinting hopefully up at Mum. She'd tried asking for Choc in her room before, but Mum hadn't liked the idea. If it was just for the holidays, though. . . She'd rather share a room with Choc than Lara, any day. But she'd settle for both.

Lara bounced up and down on her bed excitedly. "Yes, yes! Please, Mum!"

Choc danced over to her, dropping his blanket and licking her bare toes lovingly.

Lara pulled her feet back up on to the bed with a squealing giggle, and Amy laughed too.

"Well, I suppose. . ." her mum started to say, smiling at them all, and Amy hugged her. (Carefully.)

"Yes! Thanks, Mum!"

"I want him on my bed!" Lara crouched down next to Choc, and he licked her ear.

"He can choose," Amy said hurriedly. She didn't want Mum changing her mind because they were squabbling.

"Girls, you do realize. . ." Mum trailed off, and then started getting up, as if she'd changed her mind about what she was going to say.

"What?" Amy bounced up to help pull. "What is it?"

"Thank you, sweetheart." Mum looked down

18

at her worriedly. "When the new baby comes –
it'll need somewhere to sleep."

"Won't the baby go in your room? In the
Moses basket?" Amy asked slowly.

"Maybe for the first few weeks," her mum
agreed. "But we need to get the room ready. Put
the cot somewhere."

Lara looked up at her and frowned.
"Somewhere where?"

"The smallest room. Your room, Lara," Mum
said gently. "Amy's room is really big. There's
room for both of you."

"There isn't!" Amy shook her head, her eyes
panicky. There just wasn't!

Her lovely bedroom. Full of Lara. How was
there going to be any room left for her?

2

The sea had changed when they went down to the beach later that afternoon. The faint hint of blue had gone, and the water was now a dull khaki colour, muddy and sullen-looking. It looked how she felt, Amy thought. How was she ever going to share a room with Lara? And how could she have been so stupid and not realized it would happen? Babies were small, but they took up an awful lot of space. And attention.

Lara had actually been born on the day that Amy was starting school, so that a friend from down the road had to take her. No one had even asked what school was like when she got home;

they just wanted to tell her about her new baby sister. Four-year-old Amy would quite happily have sent her back. Nine-year-old Amy was big enough to realize that probably wasn't going to happen. It didn't mean she never thought about it, though.

Still. She was going to be the eldest of three soon. Somehow that felt more important than just having one little sister. She had to be grown up about things now, or at least try to be.

Choc gave a hopeful little whine, tugging on his lead. Amy could tell he wanted to go racing off over that great length of biscuit-brown sand. She looked back at Lara, who was behind her on the cliff steps, and grinned. "Race you? Down to the sea?"

"Oooh, yes!" Lara screamed, jumping the last

two steps and dashing ahead. Amy let Choc off his lead and he barked excitedly and ran round the two girls in wide, whirling circles as they raced for the sea. Lara flung off her sandals as they ran, squeaking excitedly as she got to the water and dipped her toes in.

"I nearly won!" she told Amy.

"Choc won," Amy said, hugging her. "He's faster than both of us."

Sandmouth was a perfect place for a holiday, in hot weather at least. And it was hot – too hot for Mum, who stayed collapsed in a deckchair most of the time. But for messing about on the beach it was blissful. The first proper full day, they stayed on the beach until bedtime – just nipping back up to the cottage to go to the loo and fill up bottles of water. They even had fish and chips for dinner on the beach, eating the chips out of the paper with their fingers and then dabbling their hands in the sea. When they trailed back up the steps, Amy was so sleepy with sun and sea that she almost forgot she had to share a room with Lara again.

Sharing wasn't quite as horrible as she'd thought it would be. But Lara did talk in her sleep. She was just so noisy. She breathed, and wriggled, and grunted every so often. So did Choc, but somehow Amy didn't mind him doing it. Especially when she'd turned her light off and she could feel him lying there next to her feet. Mum had insisted that they put his basket in between the two beds, but he hadn't stayed in it for long. Amy's bed was too tempting. He wriggled closer over the course of the night, gradually working his way up the bed, so that by morning, his nose was pressed lovingly into the back of her neck.

And Amy had discovered there were some fun bits about sharing a room with Lara. She was just learning how to tell jokes – she got Dad to teach them to her, even if she didn't always understand why they were funny. She was supposed to be asleep already when Amy came up to get ready for bed, but she never was. She lay there practising her jokes on Choc, waiting for the rest of her audience to arrive. She'd had a whole lot of new ones the night before.

"Amy, where did the horse go when he got sick?"

"I don't know." (Even though she did really.)

"To the horse-pital!" Then Lara sat up, staring anxiously at her. "Was that funny? Did I get it right?"

"Yes."

"Another one. This is the *best* one, Amy."

"OK." Amy settled down in bed with her book, half-reading, half-listening to Lara chattering on.

"Why did the mushroom go to the party?"

"Why?"

"Because he was a fungi!"

Amy giggled, and Choc snorted as though he was joining in too. Lara leaned out from under her covers, walking her hands along the floor and trying to stretch over the gap between the beds. She couldn't quite reach, so she just hung out of bed upside down instead. "Amy! Why is it a joke?"

"Umm, it just is. Because fungi means mushrooms – and he was a fun guy. At a party. You see?"

"No. . ."

But did she really want to be told jokes every night? Amy wondered the next morning, lying on the sand in front of her castle. The thing was, when they got home it wasn't just going to be Lara in Amy's room. It would be all her stuff, too. Lara was obsessed with mermaids. Mermaid duvet, mermaid posters, mermaid dolls. She would even want to put up her mermaid sun-catcher in Amy's window.

Where was all Amy's own stuff going to go? Her paints, and her modelling clay set, and the gorgeous metallic pencils that she was saving for something very special? How was she going to keep all her things private and safe if Lara was in her room? Except that was the thing – it wouldn't be *her* room any more. It would be Lara's room too. They were going to have to share everything. And they'd be sharing Mum and Dad even more, when the new baby came.

Amy bit her thumbnail anxiously and stared over the sand to the water's edge, where Lara was prowling up and down. Mermaid-hunting again. Every so often, Lara would freeze and peer into the water, and Amy found herself holding her breath. Had she seen one?

There was an outcrop of black rocks to one side of the beach, breaking out from the cliffs into the water. Deep in the rocks, reddish-brown strands of seaweed swirled around the pools the sea left behind. Even Amy wanted to believe that they were mermaid hair. Lara was completely convinced. Choc was staring into the water with her, skittering back every time it came towards his paws. He still wasn't quite sure about this vast wetness. It was a lot, lot bigger than the pond in the park.

Amy smacked a handful of damp sand down against the side of her castle and flinched, watching as a little landslide shivered down. Sandcastle building had to be done carefully. She didn't build the usual kind, filling buckets and turning them upside down. She liked castles that were clever on the inside. Her castles had tunnels, and towers of flat stones, glued together with a wet-sand cement, only a tiny door hole left open. She loved wondering what might move in, after they trailed back up the stone stairs with their bags and rugs. If they lasted, under the sea, what would happen?

Choc came pottering back across the beach towards her, sniffing happily at odd bits here and there. He'd already found three crabs and a lot of smelly seaweed, and it was only nearly lunchtime. He loved the beach, even if he wasn't convinced about the watery bit.

"What's that?" Lara had followed Choc, and she was standing over Amy now, dripping. She nudged the castle with her toes.

"Don't."

"I'm not! I wasn't doing anything!"

"You were going to knock it down. You always do." Amy flapped her hands at Lara, pretty in her pink swimming costume, her fair hair trailing down her back in a damp, sandy plait.

"I'm not going to knock it down!" Lara yelled, stamping her feet and flinging her bucket on to the sand.

The fragile castle, lovingly hollowed out inside, slumped inwards silently, and Lara stared at it, and then at Amy.

"I didn't mean to," she muttered, shamefaced.

Choc backed away, sneezing and shaking his head to get the sand out of his whiskers.

Amy's eyes burned. She scrambled up, wrapping her hands under her elbows to stop herself shoving Lara. She knew, deep down, that Lara hadn't meant to. But how did she always manage to ruin everything?

Amy looked at the sunken remains of her castle, and stirred it with her foot. She stood up, glancing back over at the rug. "Mum, I'm going to the rocks. Me and Choc. All right?"

Her mum, who was wedged into a deckchair a few metres up the beach, nodded vaguely. Dad was lying on the rug, half-asleep, and he only waved. That was as good as a yes, Amy thought, patting her leg to call Choc.

"The rocks! Can I come?" Lara pleaded, pattering after her. She wasn't allowed to play on the rocks on her own, it was too dangerous, Mum said. But the rocks were the perfect place to go mermaid-hunting, and she loved them.

"No!" Amy snapped back at her. She raced off across the sand, with Choc barking beside her, ears flapping. She could hear Lara wailing about being left behind, but she didn't feel guilty. Or only a bit, anyway.

★

The rocks were warm from the sun, and everyone else on the beach seemed to have got their picnics out. Amy and Choc could explore on their own. She lay down along one flat, smooth rock and stared into the water, squinting past the sun-glare. Choc stood next to her, wafting his tail back and forth slowly as he peered into the pool.

"It's all very well being the eldest, and being grown up," Amy muttered to him. "But why's it always *my* things that get spoiled? And Mum and Dad never tell her off. They just say to remember she's little. . ."

She sighed, propping her chin on one hand and enjoying the soft roar of the waves further down the beach and the hot sun on her back. She trailed her fingers in the water and smiled as the fleshy little anemones suddenly sucked in their tentacles. They looked like jelly sweets now, stuck on to the rocks.

Amy laughed quietly as a delicate, almost transparent little fish shot past. She was sure she could see its stomach inside. She wished her friend Millie was here. She'd love it. She had a massive fish tank, and even though her fish were bright tropical ones, Amy was sure her friend would still know the name of everything in the rock pool. She'd have to tell her about it when they got back. Millie went to Brownies with her, as well as school, and they were all going on pack holiday next weekend. Dad was going to drop Amy there as soon as they got back from Sandmouth on Friday afternoon. Maybe she could take some shells back for Millie, she thought, stroking a striped shell that was stuck to the weeds just below her. But not that one; she was pretty sure it was occupied. It had definitely wriggled.

Amy yawned wearily. She pillowed her cheek on her arm and stared sleepily into the water. The weeds swirled into glistening patterns, and her eyes half-closed. She felt Choc settling down for a sleep beside her, stretching himself out over the sun-warm rock.

It almost looked like there was a mermaid in the water, though there was no such thing, of course.

Amy blinked, and the face shimmered and re-formed. Long golden-red hair, rippling as the water swirled through it. Dark, shining eyes and pale deep-water skin that hardly ever saw sun.

Light glistened on polished scales, and Amy sat up, gasping, about to scream for Lara to come quick and see. The mermaid was smiling at her, one arm reaching out to beckon her close.

Then the sun went behind a cloud, and the shining water greyed and dimmed, and it was only seaweed again, and two dark shells, and an anemone.

"Did you see that?" she muttered to Choc, her heart still racing. "It was . . . I mean, it was almost there. . ."

Choc had his nose practically in the water, and his tail was twitching.

"Did you see it?" Amy breathed. "I should have brought Lara."

Choc whisked round, hopping over the rocks, and hurried back along the sand. Amy turned to watch him gallop down the beach. Mum was still in her deckchair, and it looked like Dad was fast asleep now. But Lara was slumped on her own, halfway between the rug and the sea, arms wrapped round her knees. Amy could tell how she felt even from here, just by the way her shoulders were hunched. She shouldn't have left her, Amy thought, feeling guilty again, until she saw Choc skid to a halt in front of her. Amy watched her jump up excitedly and stumble after him.

"Did you see one?" she gasped to Amy, as she scrambled over the rocks to the pool.

"Sort of. For just a second, but I'm not sure it really was. . ." Amy looked at Lara sideways, wanting to feel as excited as Lara did, but not daring to hope it could be real.

Lara grabbed her hand and looked up at her

pleadingly. "Show me," she begged. "Where was it?"

Amy crouched down by the edge of the pool, and Lara leaned against her. Amy could feel her shaking with excitement.

"Red hair. . ." Lara whispered, reaching out her hand to stroke the feathery weeds and wobbling a little. Amy grabbed her round the waist, and Choc squashed himself protectively against Lara on the other side. Sometimes Amy forgot how little she was.

"Maybe it was just the sun, shining on the water. . ." she told Lara.

But Lara shook her head. "No," she said, quite convinced. "It's a mermaid. I can nearly see her, but she's hiding. That's all. There's too many people."

Amy hugged her
tighter, wishing she could
be as certain as Lara was.
They sat watching for ages,
Lara gasping hopefully every
time the water rippled, but it didn't come back.
At last Choc wriggled, wafted his tail against

their legs, and gave Amy a meaningful look. Sitting still was all very well for a while, but there was a whole beach full of smelly seaweed to explore.

"I suppose it's probably lunchtime," she sighed. She looked back along the beach. "Actually, Dad's getting our picnic out, Lara."

Lara stood up. She was still gazing over her shoulder at the rock pool as they picked their way over the rocks and back across the sand.

"Do you think we'll ever see one again?" she whispered to Amy.

"I don't think it actually was a mermaid, Lara," Amy began, but then she stopped. Lara wanted to believe it was. And so did she. Why couldn't it be? She swung Lara's hand and pulled her into a run along the edge of the sea. Choc ran after them barking, and eyeing the splashing water suspiciously, in case it was thinking of chasing him.

"Maybe we will. And after lunch, I'll tell you what, we'll make our own mermaid. A sand one. Look, we can use all this seaweed for hair. . ."

3

After that, Lara and Amy spent a couple of hours on each beach day stretched out on the rocks. Amy took her drawing pad and pencils, and drew mermaids, and sea-dogs, and undersea palaces, while Lara stared into the glittering water, and every so often sat up to look, and tell her how clever she was.

Lara was so certain that the mermaid was there. She didn't complain about sitting and waiting, she just dabbled her fingers in the water, and occasionally dripped them on to Choc's nose, which made him sneeze. And about every ten minutes, she would gasp excitedly, peering into the water, and Amy would leap up to see if she could whatever Lara had seen. But she could never quite catch it.

The days seemed to stretch out, long and sunny, and full of almost-mermaids. Until all at once it was the last beach trip, and the last ice cream, and the last mermaid-hunt.

"I wish we could stay here. . ." Lara said sadly, swirling one hand in the water, watching as the anemones snapped shut.

"Me too," Amy agreed, drawing tiny seahorse hair-clips on to a red-seaweed-haired mermaid.

"You've got the Brownies thing," Lara pointed out.

Amy blinked. She'd been looking forward to the pack holiday for ages, but she'd almost forgotten about it, in the dreamy sunshine of their holiday. "So I have. Tomorrow, when we get back home!"

"You get all the exciting things," Lara sighed, and Amy stared at her in surprise. Maybe there were some good parts about being the eldest.

Millie came dashing across the car park, ignoring her mum having a panic behind her, and flung her arms round Amy. "I missed you while you were away, it's been the most boring week ever." She crouched down to make a fuss of Choc, who was frisking round their feet and tying Amy up with his lead. Millie loved Choc; she came with Amy to walk him whenever she was allowed.

"I wished you were there too, 'specially while I was watching the rock pools. They were really cool; they made me think about your fish."

Millie snorted with laughter suddenly. "You'll never guess what the theme for pack holiday is."

Amy shook her head. "What? Fish?"

"Close. Under the sea. Just like your holiday."

"What do we have to do now?" Amy had never been away with Brownies before. The pack holiday had always clashed with her family going away.

"Oh, you have to tell them you're here, then find your room and put your stuff away."

"We're together, aren't we?" Amy asked anxiously, but Millie sighed. "No. I asked why, and Brown Owl said they were trying to mix the ages up so all the rooms had some older ones in. You'll be OK, though. You've got Lucy and

Cassie in your room. I've got to share with loads of the little ones."

Amy wrinkled her nose. Sharing. While she was away this weekend, Dad was going to move everything out of Lara's room and into hers. Theirs. When she got home, everything would be different.

"Amy, I just need to give all the forms to Brown Owl, and then I'll be off, OK?" Dad passed over her sleeping bag and rucksack. "Give me Choc's lead. Have a great time. I'll come and pick you up on Sunday afternoon. Maybe bring your mum and Lara, if your mum's feeling up to it."

Amy hugged him goodbye, her heart suddenly a panicky race. She'd been looking forward to this weekend for ages, since they'd first brought the letters home. For weeks and weeks she'd been thinking how much fun it was going to be. But now she didn't want her dad to go. Even though Millie was here, and lots of her other friends. As her dad walked back to the car with Choc, waving goodbye to her, she wanted to run after him and beg him not to leave.

Amy bit her lip to stop herself calling after him. She couldn't work out what was the matter with her. It was only a weekend. She'd been on sleepovers before – she'd stayed at Millie's house loads of times. So why was she getting all wobbly now?

Luckily, one of the older girls who helped out, Lulu, came past just then, and gave Amy a hug. "You look so brown, Amy! Did you have a good holiday?"

Amy nodded. "Yes. It was brilliant," she added, almost surprised at how much she meant it. It really had been, and mostly because she'd got on with Lara.

"If you take your stuff upstairs fast, you two can come and help me get snacks ready for everyone. Brown Owl's brought these weird seaweed crackers because of everything being Under the Sea, but don't worry, I told her to get some proper crisps as well. . ."

Amy sat huddled up on the top bunk, hoping all the others were asleep. It was late, really late. One of the mums who'd stayed to help had been in to check on them all ages ago, in her pyjamas. Even the leaders had gone to bed. Amy was probably the only person left awake. She sniffed. If everyone was asleep, no one was going to hear her crying like a baby. She'd been determined she wouldn't, but now she couldn't help it.

She hadn't had time to miss home the night before – it had been exciting, their first night all together in a big room. They'd worked out a code with Millie's room next door, banging on the walls to send messages, although it didn't work very well, and they kept having to send one of the little ones to nip next door and ask what the message actually said. But that just made it funnier. Especially when Ellie had got caught by the leaders so many times that they'd rung her mum to check if she was OK, because she seemed to need the loo every five minutes.

By then it was so late that Amy had fallen asleep without really meaning to, and she hadn't had time to miss Mum and Dad and Lara and Choc at all. If only she could just go to sleep now!

She was really enjoying the pack holiday, so it was stupid that she was feeling homesick. *Stop it!* she told herself crossly, as she wondered if Mum was missing her too, and felt tears run down her chin. *Think about all the fun stuff!*

They'd been told to bring swimming costumes to the pack holiday (Mum had hung Amy's damp one out of her car window for most of the way home, because she'd been worried it wouldn't dry in time), but there wasn't a swimming pool, so no one had known why until that afternoon. Brown Owl had sent them upstairs to change, and when they got out into the garden of the holiday house, there was a paddling pool full of water, and a pile of water pistols, and a note saying that they had to find as many fish as they could. Nobody was sure what that meant, but they'd set off looking, and discovered that the leaders were all hiding around the garden, and they had even bigger water pistols. And Lulu had a whole bucket full of water bombs.

Everyone had got soaked, and it was brilliant, especially when Amy and Millie had nicked half the water bombs off Lulu while she was trying to stop another lot getting the fish she was guarding. Then they'd thrown them at Brown Owl from behind the hedge so she didn't even see them coming.

Amy sniggered, remembering, and wiped the tears on the edge of her sleeping bag.

Tonight the girls from Millie's room had crept into theirs instead, and they'd had a midnight feast, even though it was actually only nine o'clock. Everyone had brought sweets from home to share, tucked in the bottom of their bags. Cassie had told them a brilliant ghost story that someone had told her brother at school, about wolves, and a haunted loo, and a locked suitcase that made groaning noises. Everyone had been scared silly. Amy had even been thinking of telling everyone about the mermaid – it didn't feel like the others would say she was making it up, just then.

But then Millie had passed round a box of Maltesers, and they had reminded Amy of Choc when he did his big, sad, chocolatey eyes. He was probably missing her too. She hadn't wanted any Maltesers, and she'd kept quiet about the mermaid after all.

It was just then that they'd heard the leaders coming up to bed, and Millie and the others had to dash back to their room before they got caught. Everyone else had gone to sleep soon after that, but Amy couldn't. She'd eaten too many sour cola bottles, and she felt a bit sick.

Why couldn't she just go to sleep? She was going home tomorrow. Today, now, it had to be after midnight.

She was even really missing Lara. They'd spent ages that afternoon doing crafts, little bracelets with fish-shaped beads, and painting mermaid-shaped boxes. Lara would have loved it. Amy's box was carefully packed away in her bag now, ready to give Lara for her birthday.

She sighed, feeling the damp cold of tears soaking the blanket round her neck. She wanted Mum and Dad and Lara, and she really wanted Choc. Especially after having him on her bed all last week. She kept turning over and expecting to find a fat weight of dog next to her, but he just wasn't there. And there was nothing like sleeping in a room with five other people all breathing to make just one little sister a lot less annoying. She wouldn't mind about sharing with Lara, if only she could go home.

There were nice little tents outside, round ones, like mushrooms. Even that would be better than this noisy, stuffy room. She'd love a little mushroom tent all to herself. She sighed as Cassie muttered something in her sleep and turned over. People were meant to be *quiet* when they were asleep.

It was raining again. Drops hammered across the window as the wind gusted around. Amy shivered. Maybe she didn't want to be in a tent after all. Dani and Rachel and the others from the year above her and Millie, they were all outside in this.

Amy winced as the rain smacked against the windows again. She thought that was thunder too – the noise wasn't quite loud enough to be sure. It was horrible out there. She was definitely changing her mind about a tent.

"Amy, are you awake?"

"Yes." She quickly rubbed the tears off her face. It was Lucy, one of the younger Brownies, who had the bunk underneath her.

"Was that thunder and lightning?"

"Um, maybe. Oh. Yes, I saw a flash."

This time the thunder rolled around the trees and echoed over the house.

"I really hate thunder." Lucy's voice had gone squeaky, and she was sort of gasping. Amy eased herself out of her sleeping bag and climbed down the ladder to Lucy.

Lara didn't like thunder either. She was probably in Mum and Dad's bed right now. And Choc would be barking like mad. It wasn't that he was scared; he just didn't understand what the noise was.

Amy put her arm round Lucy. "Are you OK?"

"No!" The thunder growled round them again, and Lucy jumped. Somebody else was sniffling. "What's that?" Lucy shrieked as something rattled and screeched downstairs just as a massive flash of lightning lit up the room. Amy shivered.

"I don't know. . ." Amy muttered nervously, hearing a door bang further along the landing. "Let's go and see. Come on."

"I don't want to. . ." Lucy whimpered, but she didn't want to be left behind either, so when

Amy pulled, she got up in her sleeping bag like a fat purple caterpillar.

Dragging Lucy behind her, Amy pulled their door open. The dim light from the landing lit up the other girls in their room, all waking up now, and wide-eyed in the greyness.

"Oh, you're awake, girls." One of the leaders, Cassie's mum. "In that case, they can sleep on your floor."

Amy stared at the gang of damp-looking girls behind her, and recognized Rachel. "Did your tent leak?"

Rachel nodded. "I think we did it wrong," she whispered. "I just woke up and my feet were outside. I'm frozen. And my sleeping bag's soaked."

Cassie's mum was carrying a pile of blankets,

and the Guides were trailing big squashy things that looked like the sofa cushions from the room downstairs.

"I like camping indoors better anyway," Rachel muttered to Amy and Lucy, as she made herself a sort of blanket nest next to their bed. "Especially when it's pouring down at two o'clock in the morning."

"Night, then," Amy whispered, leaning over the side of the bunk. Two o'clock. It was tomorrow. Or today was tomorrow... She wasn't quite sure what she meant, but she knew it was good. Soon after breakfast she'd see Mum and Dad, and Choc, and Lara. She wouldn't even mind playing mermaids again, for the seventeen-millionth time...

4

"And when they went back to look the next morning, the tent wasn't even there!" Amy told Dad. "They found most of it in the hedge, and the Guide leader says she doesn't know what they did to it when they were putting it up, because that's never, ever happened before."

Dad nodded. "I remember waking up at Scout camp and finding I'd rolled down the slope in the night and half of me was sticking out of the tent."

"Did the thunder wake Lara up? Was Choc all right?"

Dad sighed. "I spent most of the night on

the sofa. There wasn't room for me in our bed with the amount of space Lara and your mum took up. And Choc was fine. Once he'd stopped growling at the thunder he came and slept on my feet. I was grateful, actually; it was a bit chilly downstairs." He gave a big fake shiver. "I wouldn't have wanted to be in a tent last night. I think you lot had the better deal being inside."

Amy nodded. "Yes. . . But I didn't like sharing a room with all the others. Well, I did enjoy the midnight feast; that bit was really good. But then loads of people snored."

Dad didn't say anything, and Amy glanced over at him, wondering why. "What is it?" she asked.

"Uncle Matt came over yesterday. We've moved Lara's stuff into your bedroom, Amesy."

Dad only called her that when he thought she was going to be upset. Amy stared out of the side window. They were nearly home.

"I know," she whispered. "You said you would."

"She's got her bed on one side, and all her stuff packed away. There was space in your wardrobe, and the drawers, so we didn't have to move Lara's ones in. We moved your dolls' house over a bit, but you'll still be able to get at it."

Amy nodded, and swallowed. She hadn't even thought about the dolls' house. She and Mum had painted the walls, and made so many beautiful things for it – they were even working on making an armchair right now. Mum was going to get some special modelling clay so they could make little legs.

She had missed Lara yesterday. Sticking down

the tiny stones to make the glittery mermaid box, she'd really missed her.

"You're being very good about it." Dad sounded relieved, and Amy wondered what Lara had been like over the weekend. She smiled to herself, looking out of the window away from Dad. She could just imagine Lara clinging on to the rails of her bed like a monkey as Dad and Uncle Matt tried to lift it out of her bedroom.

As soon as Dad unlocked the front door, Choc launched himself at Amy, barking like a mad thing. He was so excited he kept jumping round and round in circles, then racing down the hallway, and then galloping back to jump up and lick her all over again. "Oh, I missed you," Amy told him, catching him in mid-leap and nearly falling over. "Oof, you're so heavy. Good boy. Good boy, Choc."

"Did you have a good time?" Mum hurried out of the kitchen – or hurried as much as she could at the moment, anyway. Amy hugged her round Choc and the bump, which was quite tricky.

"Yes. But I did really miss all of you," she admitted. "Even you," she whispered to the bump.

Half of her wanted to sit down and tell Mum everything they'd done. But she had to go upstairs first and see what it was like. She hurried up the stairs, with Choc pressed against her legs, making pleased little noises to himself. He had missed her too, she could tell.

Lara's room was the first one off the landing, and Amy glanced in as she went past. It was almost empty, just Lara's scuffed pink wallpaper and her small wardrobe and chest of drawers left. Dad had brought the old cot down from the loft, and it was leaning up against the wall, in pieces. Amy gulped. Somehow the cot made the baby seem a lot more real. She could remember Lara sleeping in that cot. It had bite marks all along the top of the sides where Lara had chewed it.

The room looked so empty – because everything that should have been in there was in Amy's room. Amy stared at the carpet, and Choc sniffed at it curiously. They'd only had Choc for a couple of years, and he'd always known this as Lara's room. He didn't understand why everything had changed round. He patted his paw at one of the little marks on the carpet where the bed had been standing, and Amy frowned. Lara's bed was *huge*. She bit her lip and dragged herself along the few steps to her own door. She almost didn't want to see.

Amy's room was a large one – Millie was always telling her how lucky she was to have it. So there was room for two beds, she knew that really. If it had only been a case of two beds, it would have been fine.

Amy's desk was squashed up next to the window now, and her bookshelf was right next to her bed.

There was a thudding noise as Lara raced up the stairs. She'd been out in the garden – Amy guessed Mum had arranged that. She stopped in the doorway and gave Amy an uncertain look. As though she still wasn't sure she was allowed in.

I missed Lara this weekend, Amy told herself firmly. *I really missed her. I was homesick and I wished she was there.*

"Mum wouldn't let me put my posters up. . ." Lara told her. "She said I had to ask you where they could go. But that isn't fair, because it's my room now too." Lara pushed past Amy and flung herself on to her bed, looking up at her sister with half a smile. A sort of *you can't do anything about it* smile.

"I'm not having any of your stupid mermaid posters in my room," Amy snarled. All thoughts of missing Lara, and this not actually being her fault, disappeared. It was the smile that did it. It was the same smile Lara used when she was telling on Amy to Mum.

"It's our room!" Lara shouted back, bouncing

up on the bed and glaring at her. "The girls' room. Mum said so!"

Choc made a worried little noise, his tail wafting nervously from side to side. But he followed Amy as she stormed down the stairs, still dragging her rucksack and sleeping bag.

Her mum was standing at the bottom, as though she'd been just about to come and see what was going on.

"Amy? What is it? What happened?"

"I'm not sharing a room with Lara!" Amy yelled. She was tired of being nice to her mum because of the baby. No one was being nice to *her*. "I won't! I want my room back!"

Dad came out of the kitchen, looking annoyed. "Amy, you know we can't do that. The baby—"

"I never wanted there to be a baby! Why should I have to give up my room?" Amy almost faltered as she finished saying it. She knew what a horrible thing it was to say, especially when her mum was so tired. But she couldn't help it. No one cared what she thought. They just moved her out of the way, like all her stuff.

She straightened up, shaking her hair out of her eyes, and glared at her dad. "I never wanted Lara either, and I hate her, and I'm not sharing!"

"Amy!" her mum whispered in a hurt voice, and someone made a little whimpering sound from the top of the stairs.

Lara was listening.

"She doesn't mean it, Lara," her mum started to say.

"Yes I do!" Amy yelled. "Why do you always take her side?"

"Go out into the garden!" Dad snapped angrily. "I don't want to see you right now, Amy, I'm too cross. Out! And don't come back till you're in a better mood."

"Fine!" Amy hissed back, stamping through the kitchen with Choc trotting after her, his feathery tail waving as he saw her struggling with the back door. The garden meant Amy was going to play with him.

But she didn't. She sat down on the edge of the patio, crying. Choc nosed her hopefully a couple of times, but she didn't get up, so eventually he sighed heavily and sank down beside her, with his nose on her foot.

"They hate me now," Amy muttered. "It's not

fair. I wish I lived somewhere else. I wouldn't care where."

But I could go somewhere else, she thought, sitting up a little straighter and putting her chin in her hands. *I could go away, and then they'd be sorry. Wouldn't they?*

She looked down at the sleeping bag and rucksack she'd dumped on the grass. She had everything she needed. Even some food – Millie had told her there'd be a midnight feast at the pack holiday, but everyone had brought so much, they'd never eaten her stuff. She had a packet of iced ring biscuits and some cola bottles. A big bag. And her purse was in the front pocket of her rucksack. Mum hadn't been sure if she might need it.

Amy got up slowly, looking back at the

kitchen window. No one was there to see her. Mum and Dad were probably sitting on the stairs cuddling Lara and telling her that her nasty big sister didn't mean it.

"I did," she muttered, glancing up at her bedroom window. With Lara's stupid pink mermaid sun-catcher hanging in it. Amy snorted and flung her rucksack on. She almost slammed the back gate against the wall, but she caught it at the last minute. If it banged, Dad would come out to see what was going on.

Choc whined at her anxiously. He knew he wasn't supposed to go out of the garden. He had, a couple of times, before Dad put wire netting across the bottom of the fence panels. The people down the road had brought him back the first time, saying they'd found him staring into their guinea pig hutch. The second time, Amy and Mum had found him sitting in the park, watching the children in the playground. Amy had thought he hadn't really wanted to come back with them. He kept looking back and whining, and his whiskers were covered in biscuit. He was very good at looking starved. He was also very good at being loud. If she went off without him, he'd bark. . .

"Come on, Choc," Amy whispered, patting her trousers – she didn't really want to run away in her Brownie uniform, but she could hardly go back in and change, could she? "Choccie, here boy. I wish I'd got your lead. You'll have to be good. And I'll hold your collar for the roads."

She scurried down the side path to the front

of the house, creeping down the little drive on the far side of the car in case they saw her from the hallway. Then out, on to the pavement, whispering to Choc, "It's OK. Come on." He seemed to know they were doing something they shouldn't; he kept casting anxious glances back towards the house.

They got to the corner of the road when Amy suddenly realized that she didn't know where they were going. She stood hesitating by the wall, her fingers curled in Choc's collar. She hadn't really meant to bring him – but she was glad she had. His fur was soft and springy under her fingers, and he was so warm. "Where shall we go?" she muttered.

Choc pulled her gently to the edge of the pavement and looked up, his eyes hopeful.

Amy laughed. "You want to run away to the park?" Actually, it wasn't that stupid an idea. It was a big park, and the playground where they'd found Choc that time before was huge, with all sorts of climbing frames and tunnels. There was bound to be somewhere she could hide out for a bit. And it shouldn't be too busy by now. It was late afternoon.

Choc hurried her eagerly towards the park, and Amy wished she'd brought her coat. People kept looking at her Brownie uniform. She didn't want anyone to notice her. It was no good running away if someone told Mum and Dad where she was and she had to go home after half an hour.

They'd probably seen that she was gone by now, she realized, checking her watch. Dad would have gone to call her back in.

Amy slowed down, shifting her rucksack on her shoulder. Somehow, it all seemed a bit more serious now. As though she hadn't really run away until someone knew she'd done it.

Choc looked back at her curiously and barked. He wanted to get to the playground. Dogs weren't actually allowed in it, but there were usually plenty of people riding bikes or scooters round the paths at the edge, and most of them had food for a soulful-eyed dog.

The playground wasn't as empty as Amy had hoped it would be. A couple of mums were pushing little girls on the swings, and there was a gang of boys skateboarding over on the side. They were a bit older than Amy. The two mums kept giving them dirty looks, and making loud comments about playgrounds being for children.

With them there watching, there was no chance of sneaking Choc into the playground, as Amy had meant to, and she was forced to come up with another plan. A patch of

bushes and brambles ran along the back of the playground, and they walked round it as Amy eyed it thoughtfully. Choc sniffed around under the bushes with interest: the ground smelled of squirrels, and other small and delicious things.

It didn't look particularly comfortable for hiding out in, Amy decided at last. It was a bit scary, the thought of huddling up in her sleeping bag under those bushes. And prickly. And what if there were foxes?

She jumped as one of the little girls inside the playground raced along the bridge of the climbing frame, shrieking as her friend chased after her. Amy watched them dash by. The climbing frame was a massive one with all sorts of platforms and tunnels, and a couple of the little bridges ran over the back fence and out on to the grass in front of the brambly bit. The ends of the bridges had been blocked off, so that smaller children didn't use them to run out of the playground. But it would be quite easy to wriggle up on to them. Even Choc could do it if she gave him a boost.

The two little girls were playing on the seesaw now, so Amy quickly stuffed her rucksack and sleeping bag up on to the bridge and then picked up Choc. He wriggled in surprise, and she staggered. He wasn't a huge dog, but he was heavy. "Come on, up, Choc!" she muttered, trying to squish him under the metal side-rails of the bridge. Choc scrabbled indignantly but clambered on, and then whisked round to poke his nose out under the rails, as if to ask her what on earth they were doing.

"It's all right, I'm coming too." Amy hauled herself up and rolled sideways on to the bridge. "Come on." She snapped her fingers, and he scurried after her down the sloping bridge to the little turret at the end of the climbing frame.

"Look, it's perfect, you see," Amy murmured to him. "No one can see us. The rain won't get in it, and it's just about big enough to stretch out in my sleeping bag." She set the rucksack down in the corner of the dusty little space and sighed. It was a bit gloomy. Running away felt as though it ought to be more exciting somehow. She unzipped her rucksack. Maybe a biscuit would help.

Choc sniffed his way around the edge of the little room, and then put his nose out of the little doorway. He saw no reason to stay inside, and the two little girls were sitting on a bench not far away, eating raisins. He liked raisins.

"Choc, no!" Amy hissed as he set off, tail wagging, and head held sideways in his trademark shy-but-starved-dog pose. She lunged for his collar and grabbed him back. "Look, it's OK, you can have one of my iced rings. You have to stay here. You aren't allowed in the playground. No dogs."

Choc gave her an affronted look – Amy didn't usually grab at him like that. But he accepted an iced ring delicately, crunching it between his teeth, and then nosed hopefully at Amy for another.

She handed it to him without really looking. She was peering out of the doorway, wondering if the two mums had spotted him. They would be just the kind of people who'd make a big fuss. She could sort of see why; he wasn't supposed to be there. But he wasn't doing any harm.

"What are you doing?"

Amy jumped, and almost hit her head on the wooden door frame. The boys with the skateboards were on the wobbly bridge that was the other way to her turret, staring down at her.

"Nothing," she stammered, trying not to look behind her at Choc, who was sniffing inside her rucksack. He could probably smell the cola bottles.

"Give us a biscuit," one of the boys demanded.

Amy wanted to say no – those biscuits were her dinner. But she didn't dare. She stood up and held up the packet to him, but he took the whole thing, passing them all round his mates and smirking at her. Then he threw the empty plastic tray back down. "Thanks!" he told her, and the rest of them snorted with laughter and went stomping off, jumping up and down across the rope bridge as though they were trying to shake one another off.

Amy gulped. She could feel her eyes filling with tears, and she didn't want them to see her crying. She ducked back inside the little turret, but it didn't feel as safe any more. Maybe she should find somewhere else. She stuffed the empty tray back into her rucksack, and then gasped.

Where was Choc?

5

Amy burst out of her hiding place, scrabbling at her rucksack and sleeping bag. Where was he? He must have slipped out while those boys were nicking her biscuits. She stopped worrying about the two fussy mothers and ran out into the middle of the playground, shouting, "Choc! Choc!"

The boys hooted with laughter at her, but then one of them dropped down from the metal rings and pointed. "Are you calling your dog? Was that him?"

Amy whirled round and saw a small dark shape disappearing across the park, back towards the pond. "Yes! Thanks!" she called, waving to the boy as she scrambled up the sloping path after Choc. Her sleeping bag was coming out of its stuff-sack and trailing along the ground, but she couldn't stop to sort it out. She couldn't actually see Choc any more now. He must have vanished into the trees around the pond.

But by the time she got there, breathless, the pond was deserted, apart from the ducks. Amy stared out across the water anxiously, waiting for the ducks to launch themselves off the water with a flurry of furious quacking. That was usually what they did when Choc got too close.

The ducks were swimming calmly across the water – there wasn't a dog in sight.

Her heart thumping, Amy ran right round the pond, calling for Choc and peering into the clumps of reeds. What if he'd fallen in? He could have chased the ducks and gone in, easily. What if he'd drowned?

Amy started to cry. She knew she was being silly, but the light was fading a bit now, and the trees were shadowed. The quiet, still water was making her feel shivery. It was the sort of place for fairy tales. Maybe a swan princess had lured Choc into the lake with bits of bread. He loved bread.

"This is stupid!" Amy hissed at herself, and turned away from the water. If Choc wasn't by the lake, it was because he was somewhere else in the park. She hurried back along the lake path, to where she could get a clear view of the park.

It was so big, she realized anxiously, as she came out from between the trees. That was why it was Choc's favourite walk. There was so much space to run. But then usually Dad was there, and Choc did what Dad said, even if he was off the lead. He didn't get lost for Dad. Amy swallowed. She'd *lost* Choc.

She sniffed, sinking down on the grass and staring out over the park. What was she going to do? Should she wait, and hope Choc would find her? Maybe he'd already gone back to the playground, looking for her. Probably those mums chased him away, she thought, brushing hot tears off her face. She wanted to go home and get Dad, but she couldn't leave Choc. What if he got confused and went out of the park and just got even more lost? What if he got run over? Amy gasped and put her hands over her mouth.

She had almost forgotten about running away. It didn't really matter. She couldn't care less if Lara was in her room, as long as Choc was at home with them too.

If she ever found him, that was. Amy buried her face in her arms, tears soaking through to her T-shirt. She was so upset that she didn't hear the thudding of approaching paws, so she was completely unprepared when Choc leaped at her. He knocked her over backwards and landed on her stomach. Then he licked her ears lovingly.

"Choc! Where did you go? I thought I'd lost you. Stop licking! Oh! Dad!"

She hadn't noticed at first that Choc had his extending lead on, and Dad was on the other end of it, running towards them.

"Get off her, Choc." Dad pulled gently, and

Choc hopped off Amy and ran around her in circles. He was obviously very proud that he'd found her.

"Did you come looking for us?" Amy asked hesitantly.

Dad shook his head. "Mum and I had just worked out that you weren't sulking in the garden somewhere when Choc dashed in through the back gate. He wouldn't stop barking, and he kept running up and down the side path round the house. In the end I got his lead and followed him." He stared down at Amy, still sitting on the grass. "Mum said I was being stupid. She reckoned you were still hiding in the garden. She said you wouldn't have done anything as silly as run off with Choc."

"Sorry. . ." Amy whispered. "I shouldn't have

done it. I don't mind sharing with Lara really. I mean, I do mind. But I know I have to. I won't argue about it. I ran away because I was so cross, but then I thought I'd lost Choc, and it just didn't matter."

Dad pulled her up. "I can understand you don't want to share." He sighed. "I used to share a room with Uncle Matt, you know. I could have killed him half the time. But there were good bits too. It can be fun, having someone else to share a room with."

Amy nodded. "I suppose."

"It's hard for Lara too," Dad pointed out.

Amy scrunched up her nose. She didn't think so. It wasn't the same.

"And she was really upset that you said you hated her. She thinks you're so big and clever,

Amy. She just wants to be like you."

"But I don't want her to be like me! I'm me!" Amy said.

"Mmm. Anyway. She says she's not sharing a room with you any more."

Amy frowned. "Where's she going to go, then?"

Dad sighed. "Wait and see."

"How long has she been under there for?" Amy whispered.

"Pretty much since you left," Mum said quietly. She was still looking upset, and Amy felt really guilty.

The kitchen table was covered in a spotted oilcloth, which made it easier for wiping things up. The cloth was quite long, so it hung down all around, like a tent.

Amy crouched down in front of it. "Lara. . ."

There was only silence in answer, but it was a listening sort of silence. Amy wondered whether to lift up the cloth. "Can I come in?"

There was a pause as Lara considered her answer, and then she said, "No. This is my room now."

Amy felt surprisingly hurt. Usually Lara loved it if she joined in one of her games.

Choc came over from his water bowl and stuck his head under the table, looking at Lara interestedly. Most of the time, under the table was his place, and he did well out of what the girls dropped – accidentally or on purpose. He was a very useful way to get rid of vegetables.

He scooted in, wagging his tail happily, and Amy ducked under the cloth to watch him.

Choc sat down next to Lara, and then eased his front paws down straight so that he was lying flat. Lara had the cushions off the sofa under the table with her, and it looked quite comfortable. She had some books, and a couple of dolls, and an apple, and her toy first-aid kit. She seemed prepared to live under the table for a while.

"I'm going to unpack," Amy said. She took a deep breath and then added, in her nicest voice, "Do you want to come and show me where things are in our room?"

"It isn't all that big," Lara said, rather coldly. "You'll find everything."

"Oh. All right." Amy straightened up, feeling as though she'd done her best. Choc didn't come with her. He was snoozing comfortably next to Lara instead, and Amy went upstairs feeling quite lonely.

Once she'd put all her stuff away and changed out of her Brownie uniform, she sat down on her bed, looking around the room. She still didn't like it. But maybe it wasn't as bad as she'd thought. It was big enough that there was a definite Lara side and an Amy side. Their stuff wouldn't have to be all mixed up.

In fact, they could each have their own tiny little room. . . There was a thudding of paws on the stairs, and Choc nosed the door open. He nudged Amy with his nose as he padded past and then flumped down on her sleeping bag, which was still in a pile at the bottom of her bed.

Amy pursed her lips thoughtfully, remembering her Brownie holiday and those damp tents out on the field, and thinking hard.

Then she picked up the mermaid box as a peace offering, and went back downstairs.

She lay down on the floor and pushed the box under the table with the end of a wooden spoon – so Lara couldn't even say she'd put a finger into her room.

"What's that for?" Lara asked suspiciously.

But Amy could see that she was itching to pick it up. Choc sniffed at it and Lara twitched, as though she was worried he might hurt the box.

"It's for you. To say sorry for being mean. I thought you'd like it. It's a mermaid. I made it. I was going to save it for your birthday, but. . ."

"It's nice," Lara admitted, touching the glittery paint with one finger. Amy had made it very carefully, so the mermaid had reddish-streaked hair, like the seaweed.

"Can I come in?" Amy asked again, politely.

"All right," Lara said after a pause. "For a bit."

Amy crawled in and sat on one of the cushions. It was cosy. Much nicer than climbing frame. "I like it," she told Lara.

"Me too. But I can't fit all my mermaids in,

that's all. And I might get more of them for my birthday." She scowled. "I can't have my party under the table."

Lara's birthday was in a couple of days' time, and she had been counting down the days. Ten of her friends from nursery were coming, and Mum and Dad's bedroom was a weird mixture of party stuff and baby stuff, piled on top of the wardrobe and spilling out from under the bed.

Amy nodded. "I did have an idea, about our bedroom. A way it might be better."

"What?" Lara sounded suspicious again.

"I'd have to show you."

Lara scowled. "That means I have to come out. Mum's making you."

Amy shook her head. "I promise she isn't. If you don't like it, you can go straight back under the table." She crawled out, holding the cloth up for Lara, and led her upstairs past Mum, who was pretending to straighten the picture frames in the hall.

They stopped at the airing cupboard on the landing, and Amy opened it, looking hopefully at the shelves. There was a pile of old flowery sheets that Mum never used but didn't want to get rid of, just in case. Just in case of what, she never said, but they were just the thing.

"What are you doing?" Lara asked, as Amy hurried into their room and climbed up on to the window sill, trailing a sheet behind her. "You're going to fall off!"

Amy snorted. Sometimes Lara sounded exactly like Mum. She tied one corner of the first sheet round the curtain pole, then scrambled down again. "Pass me that hair ribbon." She held out a hand for it and tied on another sheet. "Now we just have to find somewhere to tie the other end. The door's going to be in my half, but you're allowed in my tent to go in and out, I don't mind. OK?"

Lara nodded. She could see what was happening now. "Use the hooks! Those hooks Dad put up on the wall for your dressing gown and stuff. The ones Mum said were stupid, because you'd never reach them!"

Amy glanced at her admiringly. She hadn't thought of that. "That might work," she agreed in a considering tone of voice.

"I'm getting you the bathroom step, wait." Lara raced out and came back carrying the step she'd always used to get to the basin. "There! And my hair ribbons this time." She handed them to Amy. "It's almost as good as under the table," she told her seriously, looking up as Amy tied the end of the sheet to one of the hooks, dividing the big room in half. The evening sun was coming straight through the window, and they were wrapped in a soft yellowish-pink light as it streamed through the patterned sheets.

Amy nodded. "I know. And it's a lot drier than a real tent, honestly."

6

Amy woke up, and blinked in surprise at the flowery tent hanging around her bed. Then she remembered what it was for, and smiled to herself.

"Amy. . ."

"Mmm?"

"When it's my party tomorrow, can all my friends come into my tent? Are they allowed in the door?"

Amy grinned. "If they're good," she said, very seriously.

Choc rolled over on to his back with his paws in the air and yawned. Mum had tried to say that him sleeping on Amy's bed was a holiday treat, but Amy and Lara had both begged, and Mum wasn't in a mood to argue.

"Maybe we can go to the woods with Choc today," Amy suggested. If it was Lara's birthday tomorrow, that meant it was almost the end of the holidays. They were going back to school on Wednesday – it was Lara's first day in Reception. It would be nice to have an expedition to the woods before they went back. Maybe even a picnic.

Then she sighed. Except of course Dad would be back at work today, and Mum wouldn't be up for a long walk. She wasn't sure whether to want the three weeks till the baby came to go fast or slow. She wanted Mum back to normal – but from now on normal was going to mean with added baby.

The bedroom door creaked open, and her dad peered round. "Oh, you're awake."

"I thought you were going back to work today?" Amy asked, looking at her clock. It was half-past seven – usually Dad was on a train into London by now.

"I was. But your mum thinks the baby might be coming early, so I'm staying home to go with her to the hospital."

There was a scuffling sound, and Lara suddenly appeared out of her flowery tent. "The baby's coming now? But it can't!"

Dad looked puzzled. "Why?"

"It's *my* birthday tomorrow!" Lara wailed. "No one's ever going to remember my birthday if the baby has today!"

"I promise we will." Dad gave her a quick hug.

"Anyway, I'm going to go and ring Kate. Mum said she had a feeling this might happen, and she spoke to Kate last night. Mum's arranged for you two to go and stay with her while Mum and I are at the hospital, remember?"

Amy nodded. That was OK. She liked Kate – she was an old school friend of Mum's and she didn't have any children, which meant she didn't understand the rules, and believed in large bags of sweets all at once. She worked from home, drawing pictures for cards, and she had beautiful pencils and paper that she let Amy borrow. She showed her how to draw things too, sometimes. Until Kate helped, Amy had never been able to get Choc's legs right when she drew pictures of him. Kate only lived a few streets away, and she came round for coffee with Mum quite often.

"So can you pack your pyjamas, and some clothes for tomorrow maybe, in case we're not back? And some books. . ." Dad suggested vaguely, as he hurried out again.

"I don't want to go to Kate's! We can't take clothes for tomorrow, we have to be back," Lara told Amy urgently. "Tomorrow's my party, Amy! My party's here!"

"Oh. . ." Amy chewed her bottom lip. Mum wasn't going to be up for a party straight after the baby came, was she? Wouldn't she have to stay in hospital for a bit?

Dad could do it. Except . . . Dad wasn't great at that kind of thing. Like he was useless at packing. He hadn't even mentioned toothbrushes.

Amy sighed. The new baby was doing even better than Lara had. She'd been upset when Mum hadn't been able to take her to school on her first day. But cancelling Lara's birthday party would be awful.

Lara turned round, marched back into her tent, and came out again carrying the pink plastic basket that usually had her dirty washing in. It was full of mermaids, and all the other things she'd taken under the table the day before. Plus a sparkly wand and a cardigan. She looked determined. "I knew I'd have to get back under there. Tell Dad I'm not going," she said to Amy as she stomped past.

Amy stared after her admiringly. It was actually a better plan than running away. Staying put. . .

"Dave!" It was Mum, sounding worried. Amy got out of bed and went out on to the landing. "Are you OK, Mum?"

"Oh, Amy. It's all right. Don't worry, but can you tell Dad we need to go soon?"

Amy swallowed nervously and hurried downstairs to find Dad. Choc galloped after her. His tail was wagging very slightly, the way it did when he wasn't sure what was going on and he hoped everything was all right. No one had put his food down yet, so he went to sit by the bowl, sniffing at it hopefully.

Dad was checking a list from the hospital that was up on the kitchen notice board while he was on the phone to Kate. When he saw Amy he rolled his eyes at the table, and she nodded.

"Mum says you have to go really soon," she told him.

"Hang on," Dad said into the phone. "What, *now*?"

Amy looked at him worriedly. "She sounded like she meant it."

"Lara, you have to get out of there!" Dad was sounding stressed. "Amy, go and get dressed."

"I'm not coming out," Lara said very clearly, from under the table. "I'm staying here, because I want to have my party."

Dad let out a strangled sort of groan. "Kate, look, Martha says it's happening now, and the girls aren't ready. Could you come over here, by any chance? Take the girls back with you? Or . . . er . . . maybe stay?" He listened hopefully, and Amy slipped under the table with Lara. It was

weird, hearing plans being made. Dad hadn't
mentioned anything about the party. She put
an arm round her little sister, and Choc pushed
his way under the tablecloth, his tail trailing.
He could sense that things weren't right – and
still he hadn't had any breakfast. Amy put the
other arm round him. He was so warm, and
she could feel his heart beating.

Lara was crying.

"I hate this baby," Lara
sniffed. "It's messing
everything up."

Amy nodded. She suddenly felt sorry for Lara. Her little sister was the same age now that Amy had been when she was born. And she wasn't going to be the baby any more.

"Don't worry," Amy whispered. "It'll be fine." She felt better saying it, although she wasn't entirely sure how she was going to make it true.

Mum's friend Kate arrived ten minutes later, panting and wearing her T-shirt on backwards. Practically as soon as she got in the door, Mum and Dad went out of it.

"We'll be back soon," Mum called, a bit shakily. "Tomorrow. Have a nice time with Kate. Be good!"

Amy came out from underneath the table to hug her, but Lara wouldn't, so Mum just blew kisses under the oilcloth.

Then the door slammed, and the house was suddenly silent again.

Amy stood in the kitchen looking at Kate, who sighed and sat down on one of the kitchen chairs, looking a bit lost.

"Did you have breakfast?" Amy asked her helpfully. "We haven't. And Dad didn't feed Choc." She pointed to the bag of dry food on the counter. It had to be kept out of Choc's reach. He could open cupboards, if there was anything interesting in them.

"No, me neither. Good idea." Kate filled Choc's bowl, and then started opening cupboard doors. "Cereal? Toast?"

"Toast," said a small gloomy voice from under the table.

"Why is she. . . ?" Kate whispered, as she dropped slices of bread into the toaster.

"Because the baby's stealing her birthday. Her party's tomorrow. Are we going to have ring everyone and tell them not to come?" Amy whispered back.

Kate sucked in a breath. "I'm guessing that wouldn't be popular."

Amy sighed. "She's got to come out the day after. It's her first day at school. But she might just go and find a table to sit under there. Lara wouldn't care if a teacher told her off. You know how stubborn she is."

"Your mum might have mentioned it." Kate looked over at the table and sighed. "She left me a list, and she did say something about the party, but I didn't realize it was tomorrow, and she was a bit occupied." She riffled through the sheets of paper she'd put down on the counter. "Mmm. OK. I need to read through all this – but toast first. Lara, are you coming out for breakfast?"

Lara didn't say anything. A small hand appeared from under the oilcloth instead.

"I suppose not." Kate handed her a plate. A china one, Amy noticed, which just showed she wasn't used to people eating under tables.

Lara wouldn't come out after breakfast either, even when Kate announced that she thought they should have a duvet day, and curl up on the sofa and watch a film, while she read through the list Amy's mum had left. She stuffed Lara's duvet under the kitchen table and turned the sound up a little bit for her, but that was all. Amy was impressed. Mum would have made far more fuss.

7

Pretending not to notice that Lara was under the table seemed to work. Lara was stubborn, but she didn't like being ignored. She appeared in the middle of the film, wearing her duvet like a cloak and scowling.

"Hello." Kate eyed her thoughtfully. "I'm glad you've come out. It would have been difficult to fit you and Amy and ten friends under the table. Especially for musical bumps."

"I can still have my party?" Lara squeaked. Choc woke up and stared at her, as though he thought she'd turned into something small and furry that he ought to be chasing.

"It won't be exactly the same as if your mum was organizing it," Kate warned her. "I've never done a party before. I might do things wrong."

Lara hugged her. "That's not your fault, Kate. I love you. It was that stupid baby." She dropped the duvet and smiled at Amy. "I was right. I told you we had to stay here because of the party."

Amy opened her mouth to argue, and then didn't. Lara probably was right. If they'd gone to Kate's house like they were supposed to have done, she had a feeling the party might not have happened.

It was a weird day. Kate was doing her best to keep them busy, putting on DVDs, drawing mermaids with Lara, helping Amy sort out her rucksack for school on Wednesday. But every so often, Amy would stop and wonder how Mum was doing. Whether they had a brother or sister yet.

Dad called at lunchtime to say that everything was fine – but it was still going to be a while. Amy felt as though she couldn't settle down to doing anything in case something happened. She kept starting things – picking up books, or drawing a few lines of a picture – and then she'd drift away, wandering around the house looking lost. It was actually a relief to go to bed, even though she was sure she'd never get to sleep.

For once, Lara was actually happy to go to bed – the sooner it was bedtime, the sooner she woke up and it was her birthday.

Kate was sleeping on the sofa downstairs,

and it was strange being upstairs with only Lara. Amy lay curled on her side, listening to Lara's whistly breathing. She was actually glad her little sister was there. The house felt odd, and far too quiet.

Eventually, Amy gave up trying to sleep, and turned her bedside light on. Choc opened one eye and watched her thoughtfully, as if he was trying to work out if this meant breakfast. He obviously decided not, as he wriggled further down the bed away from the light and stuffed his head under his fleece blanket. Amy murmured, "Sorry, go back to sleep," at him, and reached for her pencils. She was thinking she might make a birthday card for Lara – Mum had bought one for her to use, ages ago, but she was feeling sorry that the baby had taken all the glory out of Lara's day. Dad would have called Kate if anything had happened; they'd made him promise. So the baby was going to come on Lara's actual birthday. She deserved a really good handmade card.

"Amy. . ."

Amy jumped. Lara hadn't been talking, so she'd just assumed she was asleep.

"What?" she squeaked, and the fleece blanket wriggled crossly. "Sorry, Choc. Are you OK?" she hissed at Lara.

"I can't sleep," Lara said sadly, appearing at the edge of the sheet dividing the room. "Can I come in your bed?"

Amy stared at her. She'd forgotten that if Lara had a bad dream she still went into Mum and Dad's room, and then fell asleep in a star shape, taking up as much room as she possibly could.

"My bed isn't big enough for you and me and Choc. I've got a better idea. Get your duvet and your pillow."

"Are we going back under the kitchen table?" Lara asked.

"No. We're making a nest. Put your duvet on the floor – here, look." Amy fluffed the duvet up artistically into a nesty sort of shape, and Lara flumped into it happily.

Choc appeared at the edge of Amy's bed, standing there looking down curiously at what the girls were doing. Then he leaped enthusiastically on top of Lara to join in. He overshot slightly, tangled himself in the end of one of the flowery sheets, and wriggled madly, ears flapping.

"Choc, careful," Amy tried to whisper, but she was giggling too much to get the words out. "Ssshh! You'll wake Kate. Keep still, Choc! Oops."

The sheet came untied from the hair ribbons and flumped down on top of Choc. He looked like he was in a nativity play, being a shepherd in a sheet with just his furry nose sticking out.

"Well done, Choc. We can make them part of the nest." Amy untied the other sheet from the curtain rail and wrapped it round Lara and Choc. Then she pulled her duvet and pillow down from her bed and wrapped herself up in a sort of sausage next to them. She didn't mind that the tent had gone. It didn't seem such a problem, having Lara in her room any more.

Lara was warm, almost too warm on such a hot night, and the duvet nearly softened the floor enough to make it comfortable. Amy yawned, and turned her light off, her thoughts fuzzing over with sleep.

"Sausages. Biscuits. Crisps. Cheese and jam sandwiches—"

"Cheese and jam?" Kate looked up from the party food list, her face horrified.

"She means cream cheese," Amy pointed out. "Cream cheese and jam. Mum makes them for her. It's disgusting, but not as disgusting as, like, cheddar and jam would be. . ."

"Oh." Kate nodded, looking slightly relieved. "All right, then. We can have plain jam as well, maybe. Go on, Lara. Anything else?"

"Sausages," Lara said thoughtfully. Choc closed his eyes blissfully and leaned against her. He knew what sausages were.

"Already got those."

"*More* sausages." Lara nodded. "Pizza slices. Oh, and cake! Birthday cake! It's going to be a mermaid, Mummy's making it for me, she said. . ." Her voice trailed off, and a worried expression crinkled round her eyes. "Mummy said. . ."

Kate sighed. "I don't think she'll be able to, Lara. You heard how tired she sounded on the phone, didn't you? And she's got to be at the hospital a little while longer."

Lara's worried expression deepened into a full-blown scowl. Dad had called early that morning – early enough to have woken them all up. Kate had brought the phone upstairs and handed it to Amy in their nest of bedding.

Dad was very excited, and he didn't really seem to know what time it was. He wanted to tell them that they had a baby brother. Amy wasn't sure if she was excited or not – Dad had sounded so happy, and she'd caught a little bit of that – but Lara definitely wasn't.

Even when Dad had said they could both help choose the baby's name. It was just like she'd said would happen – the baby had stolen her birthday. When Dad had said that he was like a really special present, Lara had not looked impressed.

Then Dad had passed the phone to Mum to say hello. Kate was right – she'd done her best to make a fuss of Lara on her birthday, promising that there would be lots of presents later. But she sounded exhausted, though she'd promised Amy she was absolutely fine. She definitely wasn't up to mermaid-birthday-cake making.

Kate put an arm round Lara rather uncertainly, especially when Lara stayed stone still with her arms folded. "We'll buy a birthday cake in the supermarket when we get all the other things," she said reassuringly. "I know it won't be as special as one your mum made, but it'll still be nice."

"Can't you make one?" Amy asked.

Kate shook her head slowly. "I wouldn't know how, Amy. I've never made a birthday cake for anybody."

Lara was still looking grumpy, but she nodded. "Mum's really good at cakes. Don't forget sausages," she muttered, eyeing Kate's list.

Amy shoved her hands in her pockets and wondered if she could pretend she didn't belong with Kate and Lara. No one would believe her, though. She and Lara looked too alike, even when Lara was scarlet from crying.

Kate was kneeling on the floor of the cake

aisle next to Lara. "Lara, look. I know you're not happy. But they don't do mermaids. And the man on the bakery counter said they couldn't make one before this afternoon. I'm really, really sorry."

"She promised!" Lara wailed.

"You have to choose one of these," Kate explained. "Princesses?"

"The pony one's nice. . ." Amy suggested.

"Caterpillar," Lara sniffed. She wasn't that into ponies.

"Really?" Kate blinked, but she didn't argue. "Fine. Let's go and pay for all this lot."

Kate drove them back home, and then vanished out into the garden – that was where most of the party was going to be, according to Mum's plan. The weather was on their side.

Amy was wearing shorts and a vest top, and she was still too hot. In fact, it was almost the nicest weather they'd had all summer, now.

Mum had arranged for a man to come with a bouncy castle for the party, and Kate was watching him set it up while she put out a table for tea and hung up balloons. She looked hot, and a bit panicked.

Amy leaned on their bedroom window sill, watching the castle grow – it was funny, the way it kept wobbling. Choc wasn't sure about it at all. He was standing next to Amy on the chair from her desk, his paws on the window sill, growling a low, edgy growl. Something was growing in his garden. Amy was stroking him soothingly, but he wouldn't be comforted, especially as the castle just kept on getting bigger.

She was surprised that Lara wasn't out there, bouncing up and down next to the man and asking when she could get on. Mum had arranged for him to bring it early, so that Lara could have a good go on it before her friends came.

Actually, where was Lara? She hadn't seen her since they got back from the shops.

"Where did she go, Choc?" Amy muttered to him. "Where's Lara?"

Choc cast one more suspicious look out of the window, but he obviously thought that he'd frightened the castle enough now, and it was safe to leave it in the garden. He jumped down from the chair and set off downstairs, with Amy padding barefoot after him. She followed him into the kitchen, in time to see his feathery tail disappearing under the kitchen table. Amy sighed and peered in.

Lara stared back, blinking owlishly as the sunlight poured into the dim space under the tablecloth.

"Why are you back under there again?" Amy asked, a little impatiently.

Lara sniffed and rubbed the back of her hand over her nose. She'd been crying. She still *was* crying. Amy felt guilty.

"What's the matter?"

"I wanted a mermaid cake. . ." Lara said pathetically.

"They didn't have one!"

"Kate could make one." Lara's bottom lip edged out stubbornly.

Amy sighed. "She doesn't know how. She's

never had the practice, Lara. Cakes are hard."

"Mummy promised." Lara put out a small, hot hand and grabbed the side of Amy's shorts, pulling her under the table to hug. Choc collapsed over them like a hot furry rug, and Amy stared worriedly at the wood grain on the underside of the table. Lara's friends were coming in about four hours. There was a bouncy castle, food – and a weird green caterpillar cake. Amy wasn't sure that even Kate could pull off ignoring that Lara was hiding under the kitchen table when it was Lara's own birthday party. She was going to have to do something.

8

"What are you doing?" Lara asked uncertainly as Amy pulled out one of the stools that sat round the table and carried it over to the kitchen counter.

"Looking for Mum's cake book. The party one. She always uses the same recipe; it's the one with all the sugar and stuff stuck to it."

Lara stuck her head out under the cloth, and Choc followed her – one blonde head and one furry chocolate one. "*You're* going to make me a cake?"

Amy shrugged. "I can try. There's butter and eggs in the fridge. Mum had all the ingredients ready."

"But you don't know how!"

"That's what recipes are for, Lara! Don't you want a mermaid cake?"

Lara didn't say anything. She ducked back under the table – she obviously didn't trust Amy to make the cake. For a minute, Amy wondered if she was being stupid. But she really didn't want Lara's party to be a disaster. Lara would remember it always as the time the new baby spoiled her birthday. It would be horrible. And it would upset Mum too.

If a mermaid cake would get Lara out from under the table in time for her friends to arrive, it was worth the effort.

She found the cake book and sat down at the table to read the recipe, tucking her feet back under the stool. The recipe didn't look all that difficult, and she'd helped Mum make cakes lots of times. She could do this.

"You aren't allowed to touch the oven!" Lara sang out, in a tell-tale sort of voice as Amy got up and stood next to it, eyeing the dials.

"And you're not allowed to skulk under the table because you're sulking," Amy trilled back. "I'm being careful." She turned the dials to the right temperature, and heard the oven begin to hum hopefully.

When she'd made cakes with Mum, it had seemed a bit easier than this. There were a lot of lumps. Perhaps it all melted together properly when you put it in the oven, Amy decided, staring down at the bowl worriedly.

"Are you making it?" Lara's voice came from

round her knees.

"Yes. I'm about to put the eggs in," Amy said firmly.

Lara didn't answer, but the silence from under the table was a bit more hopeful now.

Amy broke the eggs into the bowl, one at a time, with some flour. Exactly as the recipe suggested. Only the recipe didn't mention what to do if half the shell ended up in the bowl.

Amy hissed through her teeth, and tried to pick the bits out with a spoon, but they swam away from her. She would leave them, she thought. There weren't all that many. She looked nervously at the next egg.

"What's the matter?" Lara demanded anxiously, grabbing her leg. "Is it going all wrong?"

"No! It's fine. Don't whinge— Ow, Lara, don't do that, you made me spill the rest of that egg!"

"It got on me!" Lara wailed. "It's slimy! It's in my hair!"

Choc gave a little whine of excitement and started trying to lick Lara.

Lara howled.

"Amy, what are you doing?"

She jumped – Kate sounded completely horrified.

Amy stretched out a hand to the yellowish mess on the floor, and realized there wasn't a lot she could do about it with just fingers. And Choc was doing his hoover impression now, licking it up gleefully. He liked her cake, anyway. . .

Amy looked up at Kate guiltily. "I was trying – Lara still wanted a mermaid cake. She went back under the table, and I didn't think she'd come out. I was worried that if Mum came back, and we'd had to cancel the party because Lara was under the table, she'd be really upset." She gave Kate a pleading look. "Sorry about the floor. . ."

"Look at my hair!" Lara crawled out and stood up in front of Kate, her face scarlet. "Egg in it!"

"Some people put egg on their hair on purpose, to make it shiny." Kate sighed. "All right. If you want a mermaid, you can have a mermaid. It's your birthday, after all. And Amy's right, I don't want to tell your mum you wouldn't come to your own party. Come on."

She grabbed Lara's hand.

"Where are we going?" Amy asked, following them into the hall.

"We're putting a bandana on Lara, and then we're going to the corner shop."

"What are we going to do with the ones that aren't green?" Lara asked hopefully, running ever-so-casual fingers through the mixing bowl. It was full of pink and red and purple and orange sweets, and it looked like a treasure chest.

Kate frowned at the cake. "You can eat them," she told Lara. She wasn't really paying attention, as she was trying to work out how to turn one square, slightly lumpy sponge cake (Amy's creation) and one green caterpillar cake into a mermaid. She'd drawn out a plan on a piece of paper, but Amy wasn't sure how they were going to get from paper to cake.

Lara half-closed her eyes and stared at the bowl of sweets, as though she didn't know where to start. "Really all of them?" she whispered, just too quietly for Kate to hear. If Kate didn't say no, that was almost as good as if she'd said yes. . .

The other mixing bowl was full of all the green and yellow fruit pastilles that they'd picked out once they'd put the cake in the oven and scrubbed the egg out of Lara's hair. They'd bought eighteen tubes of fruit pastilles (all the newsagent's had) and a large bag of green jelly turtles, which Amy was working her way through with the scissors from her pencil case.

Once she'd chopped the little flippers off, they looked just like mermaid scales. And the flippery bits tasted even better than whole turtles, she'd discovered. She was doing two for her, one for Choc. He'd been sulking, because they didn't take him to the corner shop.

Kate reckoned that if they were clever, they could cut the caterpillar cake into a tail shape and cover it with the green sweets, and it would be just like a mermaid. They'd also bought some strawberry bootlaces. Kate said that real mermaids all had red hair. It was a fact.

Amy had nearly spilled her bagful of turtles all over the shop floor when Kate said it. A sudden picture flashed in front of her eyes – the fronds of dark-red seaweedy hair waving around the pale mermaid face in the rock pool. She'd almost forgotten, with everything else that was going on.

Amy wondered for a moment when Kate had seen a mermaid. Then Lara nodded seriously and picked up two packets of bootlaces without even trying to argue that mermaids were blonde, and Kate's face was so relieved, Amy saw she hadn't really meant it.

"All right," Kate muttered, picking up a kitchen knife and starting to cut into the sponge. "This actually looks like a nice cake, Amy, especially for a first attempt. Your mum's got lots of food colouring in the cupboard, and a gold board to put the cake on, and even some pinkish sort of fondant stuff – looks like modelling clay. I reckon she was going to use that to make the mermaid with, so we'll have a go. It's just like a big art project. . ." She smiled at her.

"Only you can eat it," Amy added helpfully. "Which is even better. Where are you going?"

Lara had suddenly scooted round Kate and dashed out into the hall, making for the loo.

"Is she all right?" Kate asked anxiously, looking from the cake to the hall and back again, as though she wasn't sure what to worry about first.

Amy sighed and held up the mixing bowl, which was empty.

Kate swallowed. "She ate *all* of them?"

"You didn't tell her not to. . ."

Lara trailed back into the kitchen, looking rather pale, and red under the eyes.

"Were you sick?" Amy asked her.

Lara nodded, and sat down on one of the stools, admiring the flourishing green tail that Kate had shaped. "I don't care. I feel fine now." She smiled faintly at Kate. "It was worth it."

Choc was sitting next to Amy, wagging his tail hopefully. Dogs were not allowed on the bouncy castle – Kate had had to sign a piece of paper agreeing to all the rules, and that had been one of them. But now that it had stopped growing, Choc was desperate to get on it, Amy could tell. He was shivering with excitement, and he kept leaning closer and closer. Then he would wriggle his paws so the rest of him caught up with his nose.

Amy was sitting next to him to hold him back. She'd had a go before everyone else arrived, and anyway the castle looked a bit dangerous now. Lara's mate from nursery, Ben, was running from one side of the castle to the other, and just ploughing through anybody who got in his way.

Kate had looked at them all bouncing and decided to change the timing plan slightly, so that tea was right at the end of the party. She said she loved Amy's mum very much, but she wasn't cleaning up a bouncy castle after ten children had been sick on it, even for her.

Amy looked at her watch. Another quarter of an hour. She couldn't wait for tea time – she wanted to see the mermaid cake in all its glory, with the candles in the sugar seashells that Kate had modelled out of the spare pink icing. Amy was so proud of it. She kept nipping back into the kitchen and sneaking little looks under the silver foil they'd covered it up with. Twice, she'd found Lara there admiring it too. The cake was probably the nicest thing she'd ever done for Lara, she thought.

She got up, clicking her fingers to call Choc to follow her. If she left him in the garden, he'd be on that bouncy castle before she'd even got in the house. Choc and Ben together would be a lethal combination.

"Ooh, Amy, are you coming to help?" Kate stuffed a plate of sausages into her hands. "Can you put that in the middle of the table for me?"

As soon as she went out into the garden again, the castle seemed to empty itself by magic.

"Is it tea now?" about three small girls asked

her, reaching for sausages.

Amy nodded, holding the sausages out of their way. "Yes. Um, Kate?"

"Oh! Sit down first. No food for anyone who isn't sitting down!" Kate ran out into the garden with more sausages and a slopping jug of squash.

"When is it birthday cake?" Lara hissed to her. "Now? Can we have it now?"

"No. You have to eat other stuff first." Kate nudged Amy. "That little girl next to Lara is licking the icing off the biscuits, and then she's putting them back!"

Amy nodded. "That's what they do at parties, Kate. Lara's doing it too, but she's feeding the biscuits to Choc after she's licked the icing. Choc, here, come here!" Amy crouched down by the party table, and Choc crept out reluctantly, looking hard done by and licking biscuit off his whiskers.

"I've finished!" Ben stood up and made for the bouncy castle, and a couple of the others got up to follow him.

"Birthday cake?" Lara asked hopefully, and Kate looked at the half-eaten food scattered all over the table and sighed and nodded, and turned back to the kitchen. "Yes, now it's all right, Lara."

Amy ran round in front of Ben and the other two, and tried to herd them back towards the table. "Don't you want to see the cake?"

The two girls went obediently back to the table, but Ben looked mulish. "No. I want to go on the castle."

146

Amy folded her arms. This was Lara's big moment. "No cake, no party bag!" she hissed at Ben.

Ben stared back, obviously trying to decide if she meant it or not.

Amy glared at him, and he ducked his head and hurried to sit down. Then she raced back to the kitchen door to see if Kate was all right carrying the cake. Choc gazed after her for a second, and then shot back under the table – he could smell the sausages.

"Oh, look at it! It looks so good. . ." Amy said happily, meeting Kate at the door. "You're Lara's favourite person for ever now, you know. You might have to make her next birthday cake as well."

"I'm going to be on holiday next September,"

Kate said firmly. "Your mum can do Lara's party and one for the baby, on the same day, without me."

Lara stood up on her chair as they rounded the corner from the kitchen door, and squeaked, "Look, look, my cake! It's a mermaid!"

"Amy, I've just thought – get my phone out of my shorts pocket!" Kate said hastily, leaning towards her and frantically trying to balance the cake. "We need to take a photo for your mum and dad, of Lara blowing her candles out."

But Amy was staring round her, into the living-room window. "No, we don't! Look! They're here!"

Her mum was waving excitedly, while Dad came behind her with the baby car seat that had been sitting in the hall for weeks. Now there was actually a baby in it, instead of one of Lara's mermaids. Choc emerged from under the tea table and sniffed at it curiously. The baby was wrapped in a blanket, despite the heat, and Choc had no idea what it was.

"You made a cake!" Amy's mum said to Kate, wide-eyed, as she came out into the garden. "I thought you were just going to buy one. It's beautiful. I never thought of using sweets on the tail."

"Well, there weren't any mermaids in the shop, so . . . we all made it. It was Amy's idea."

Amy looked proudly down at the fat green tail.

"She'd better blow these candles out," Kate said as she put the mermaid down in front of Lara, who was still far more excited about the

cake than the new baby, and Lara blew out the
candles in one pent-up breath, wobbling on her
chair.

Amy sighed and put her arm round her mum,

who hugged her back. Something inside her stomach seemed to flutter and disappear. They were back. Lara liked her cake. If Lara went back under the table, it wasn't just up to Amy to get her out. Amy looked thoughtfully at the baby. He seemed very small and reddish and quiet. Not at all as she'd expected, for someone who'd caused so much trouble.

Choc pressed against her leg, quivering with curiosity and sniffing at the thing in the blanket. Dad hitched the car seat higher up, making shhing noises, and the baby wriggled a little and went back to sleep.

"You can't lick it," Amy muttered, catching Choc's collar. "Look, cake," she added, trying to distract him, and Choc wagged his tail, thumping it happily against her bare leg.

Lara's friends stared at the cake admiringly – even Ben, who was impressed by the number of sweets all over it. The red bootlace hair glimmered in the afternoon sun, and Amy smiled. All mermaids had red hair; it was a fact. . .

"My sister made my cake for me," Lara said proudly. "Almost all by herself."

If you liked

The CHOCOLATE Dog,

try this!

Everyone thinks Penguin is a silly name for
a cat, but Alfie thinks it's perfect. To Alfie,
he's the best cat in the world.

Penguin loves to play in the overgrown garden
next door. But when a new girl moves in and
reclaims it, Alfie worries she might think
Penguin belongs to her too!

HOLLY has always loved animals. As a child,
she had two dogs, a cat, and at one point, nine
gerbils (an accident). Holly's other love is books.
Holly now lives in Reading with her husband,
three sons and a very spoilt cat.